Down With Frogs

Eden Gruger

To Nick, Mabel and Ziggy

The Curry Question

Neil offered to cook me a romantic dinner, given that the last time someone cooked me a 'romantic dinner' they ended up in A & E I wasn't as keen as you might think; anyway, he wanted to cook, so I said yes and hoped this time dinner wouldn't involve a burns unit. On the chosen evening I was greeted by an indefinable smell, it was spicy, it was sort of familiar, but it wasn't instantly recognisable, and I was mildly concerned.

Neil wouldn't let me near the kitchen, which is quite tricky in an open plan house, so I sat on the other side of the living room listening to his day with 15% of my mind still trying to work out what that smell reminded me of.

The moment arrived, the plates were coming to the table, and I saw... something blobby orange in the style of a fresh cowpat. Now, this is not a story about ha, ha, men cannot cook, they are domestic idiots; many men can create culinary masterpieces, which have their partners rubbing their hands together and smacking their lips with glee when it is their turn to cook. All I am saying is that Neil was not one of those men.

I wondered whether he had forgotten that he was cooking and so had grabbed something from the ready meal aisle and was passing it off as his own; sadly I was not that lucky. Moving the orange around I thought I saw pink... prawns? But no, there was nothing of that shape, no point trying to guess, so I ask 'what have you called your masterpiece?' 'Crabstick curry' says he proudly.

I try not to look visibly horrified and feel instantly annoyed with myself that I hadn't thought to practise my poker face lately. He had planned this meal, thinking crabsticks are very low in calories, so by definition must be much healthier than the traditional lamb, prawn or even chicken. He had bought the supermarket's cheapest own brand of curry sauce as 'they are all basically the same, aren't they?' Hence the colour and he hadn't remembered any veg but stated confidently 'I don't think it needs them'.

Holy crap, a jar of curry sauce with crab sticks, which I wouldn't eat by themselves, let alone covered in cheap sauce.

That explained why I couldn't identify the smell, crabsticks are actually made from fish, but having heard an internet rumour once that they were made of cow's intestines; I have never eaten one from that day to this, also I wasn't sure that they were supposed to be cooked.

The texture achieved was both stringy and slimy, which is definitely not something that every foodstuff could accomplish, so well done crab sticks, or should I say crabstick manufacturers.

I did pick at it, and really did try to eat some of it, but after the first forkful I knew I wouldn't be able to finish it, and didn't think throwing up on the table would be proper guest etiquette.

In the end, I had no option but to admit defeat and pleaded a large lunch, and having eaten as much as I could, he really had given me a massive portion, far more than I could manage. Neil was suspicious, having seen me barge children out of the way in McDonald's to get my post-gym Big Mac, and he knew I wasn't a 'one lettuce leaf and I am full' kind of girl.

I had to give a full five minutes praise about how inventive he was, and how much I appreciated all his efforts. Maybe I was coming down with something, and yes I did usually eat like a plague of locusts (I wasn't too happy at having to agree to this, but I needed a smoke screen to blot out my plate). And in a move, which both revolted me and excited my admiration, Neil managed to eat his own plate of food and then mine - what a trooper.

The next morning I had a text from him saying he hoped I was alright as he had been up most of the night with my stomach bug. Fortunately, he didn't seem to have passed it on to me.

Going to meet the parents – Dan

I really liked Dan, he gave me flutters in all the right places and seemed just as keen as I was, so when he asked me to come and meet his family, I was excited and didn't make too many efforts to hide it. He said everyone had been teasing him for his absences from family time and his turning up with 'kissing lips', that well-known affliction of the newly entwined; his sisters wanted to know who was the mystery woman, and his brothers wanted to know what else was red and swollen.

As the chosen Saturday approached the idea of meeting two brothers, two sisters, one sister-in-law, one partner, two brothers-in-law, five children and his mum and dad started to play on my mind.

Large families can be a real challenge, everyone knows what the rules and traditions are (except you) making it is easy to tread on toes and feelings unwittingly. I was determined to make a good impression, these people could become my family, and we would never forget meeting for the first time.

My heart was banging as we walked up the path, Thor (the dog) was going crazy behind the door, and although a dog lover I instantly knew that this would not be one of those times when I ended up on the floor tickling the tummy of the family pet. Dan's mum shouted to come around to the side gate to avoid the dog jumping all over me, telling me he wasn't vicious but 'he can be a bit funny with new people'. His brother said 'and with people he knows too, look, I still have that scar on my arm'; this didn't help to bolster my confidence.

After this nerve-wracking start things began to go more smoothly, it was a sunny day, so everyone had decamped to the garden, the nieces and nephews played in a giant paddling pool, and the adults sat around in chairs and on the lawn relaxing and chatting. I fell into the natural style of teasing and laughed at all the embarrassing stories they shared with me about Dan and he about them.

It wasn't long before I realised my bladder was full, really, really full, drinking a lot of coffee after rather a lot of bedroom action equals water infection; an undiagnosed water infection plus a very full bladder equals potential leakage. But as bursting as I was I didn't want to go into the house by myself and encounter the funny dog, he didn't know I wasn't a burglar yet, did he?

Using all my willpower I managed to ignore my urge to go to the toilet, for about another two hours until I couldn't wait any longer, and when someone else made for the house, I dashed in behind them. After the longest pee I felt considerable relief, and smiled at my own silliness; after washing my hands I turned to pick up the towel and became aware of the rest of my overworked bladder emptying itself inside my jeans.

I froze; not for the first time in my life I felt this could not really be happening, any second now someone would tap on the door and whisper it's ok, you are in your own version of the 'Truman Show', it is all a test. Sadly, there was no tap on the door and rescue from a kindly bit-part actor.

Looking down I could not decide whether the wet patch was immediately noticeable, but I quickly realised that it was going to be impossible to hide in the one and only toilet for long without raising suspicion; I began to panic. I needed to leave the bathroom and the house to change my clothes.

Tying my jumper around my waist to try and hide the evidence, I came out to find the whole family squeezed into the living room discussing pizza. I was offered a space to sit down but politely refused, I couldn't leave a wet patch on the sofa, my only option was to suggest I go to get the pizza order, so I could escape.

I left the house and sped to the nearest shop to buy a pair of trousers; giving no thought to how I would explain wearing different trousers on my return. The shop was just closing, and the lady would not take pity on me, having left the shop empty handed my panicked homing instinct cut in.

My little car sped the 10 mile round trip back to my house to change, before heading back to the house, via the pizza pick up.

By the time I arrived back people were giving me funny looks and each other micro expressions I couldn't read. One brother and his wife had left, having given me up for dead, another had gone out, and one of the sisters had got fed up and gone to the chippy, so everyone was tucking into fish and chips when I got back.

I wish I had said that my car broke down, or that I bumped into a friend and got chatting, or that the queue had been long, the pizza not ready when I arrived, or that aliens had kidnapped me. However, my frazzled brain supplied none of these, and instead, I handed over the pizza and said 'phew, sorry it took so long, I needed to pop in on my other boyfriend'.

When a surprise really is surprising

Jack had asked me to keep the weekend free as he had a 'big surprise' for me, and not being the most subtle of men he said 'this will be the best evening you have had in your life'. Now that is quite a claim having had several other very memorable evenings, and so the old imagination cogs started whirling; he told me that we were going somewhere very dressy, so I was to make an effort, that he was taking me somewhere very special, and important.

Go on, what would you be thinking? He even referred to me as Mrs Womble in conversation (this is a pseudo name, of course, there have only been three English male Womble's born in the last 100 years); understandably (I think) I was excited.

Speaking to posh Fiona she said it could only mean one thing, it was bound to be a proposal! Don't misunderstand me, I liked Jack, but his moods could be hard to manage, and I wasn't sure that I could handle being with him forever. But still, a proposal was not to be taken lightly, the least I could do was to dress appropriately for the event.

Under Fiona's watchful eye, we shopped for a pale pink, one shoulder, asymmetric dress, not the sort of thing I would have looked at usually, but Fi says stylish and sophisticated is the way to go, and she collects proposals, so I bow to her superior knowledge on this one.

She also tells me that I will need to get a blow dry, have my nails done, and wear a small, but dangerous heel 'or the dress won't work'. As she is the most assertive of my friends, I do not mention that for the dress to stop working it would have to become see-through, thereby not covering up my secret bits, or be made of ice cubes or wet towels, preventing me from being both dry and warm.

Neither malfunction could be caused by my choice of footwear, even if I wore wellies; naturally, I only think these things privately, on the outside I just nod and do as I am told.

A message from Fiona in the morning tells me not to eat bread all day, and not to eat too much of anything to make sure my belly is dress ready. Fortunately, beautification takes so much time out of the day that I don't have time to think about the sandwiches I am not eating. I get a manicure then have to sit and wait for a week to let it dry.

After getting hair done and applying makeup, I manage to dress without putting any of my shaking fingers through my tights. Even though I have fasted all day, by the time evening rolls around I can barely think about having to eat dinner, my butterflies are so huge.

The doorbell rings, I hobble down the stairs, breathe in, attach a smile and open the door; Jack's eyes nearly pop out, 'wow, you look amazing, you really made an effort, I almost didn't recognise you' he says, which I chose to hear as a compliment; he yanks me towards him to give me a passionate kiss.

It is then that I notice with a sinking feeling that he is wearing jeans and a shirt, wherever we are going it can't be that posh if he is in jeans. My butterflies pause on their manic freewheeling long enough to notice there could be a problem, they wait to see what is coming next. 'How long will it take to get there?' I ask, trying to sound breezy, 'oh' he smiles, 'don't worry, it's not far, we don't need a cab, it's an easy 15 minute walk'.

Thinking of my heels, or more accurately my feet, I look down pointedly, but he doesn't seem to notice, saying that we had better get going for our reservation.

Anyone who occasionally wears heels and never walks any further in them than from the cab to the bar stool will understand how all my thoughts were below the knee during our journey. I tell myself every painful step is a step closer to our destination, and then not only could I sit down, but I could expect 'the best night of my life'.

As my feet began to ache, then my heels to burn, and the balls of my feet started to feel like my shoes were full of tiny sharp stones, I wondered where this fancy venue was that was within walking distance.

Finally, we walked on to the high street where I knew there were some 'nice', but definitely no elegant, destinations and instantly felt like a little girl who had raided her mum's wardrobe.

With my poor feet screaming I couldn't even run away; thinking all this I hadn't noticed myself being steered into a branch of a well-known chain of French cafes.

As lovely as it was, and it was a pretty room, it could not be described as expensive or fancy; I sat down as I came down to earth – with a bump. As the waiter came over Jack said 'Would you like Champagne?' which made it even worse, there I was done up to the nines, thinking about Champagne in a café feeling like the sort of person who thinks this is a fancy night out.

The female staff look sympathetic when I accidentally catch their eyes, but this could be because Jack is behaving like he is the last of the big spenders. We get through the evening thanks to the mellowing effects of red wine.

Fortunately, Jack doesn't propose, his big news is that he has decided he wants to introduce me to his parents. Yep, that is how deluded he was, he thought that hearing that would be the best night of my life.

I realised then that Jack and I were not on the same wavelength and it was just wasting each other's time, so the next day I called him and told him it was over.

Sticks and Stones

That's not the best hairstyle for you; long hair would suit you better

That dress doesn't look right on you babe; what about the other one I like?

Have you put on a bit of weight? That top looks a bit tight.

You know I only tell you cos I care

Because I love you....

That girl isn't your real friend; she's leading you astray

That doesn't sound like the right course, job, opportunity, choice

You know it would all go wrong anyway

I'm just trying to help you

Because I love you...

Holiday? But I would miss you too much

If you went far away,

I wouldn't like you to be too far away.

Let's go together when I have the time

Because I love you.....

No one knows you the way I do

I think by now you know who's best for you

I'll show you how you should behave

To help you not make so many mistakes

Because I love you.....

You always have to start a fight

Can't you see I'm tired?

I can't even take you out without you flirting

That hurts me, and that's not fair,

Because I love you...

You're an embarrassment

Why did you say that in front of my friends?

How can you be so stupid?

Are you trying to make me angry?

You know I love you....

This place looks like shit, and so do you

Why don't you even try to make me happy?

After all the things I do for you,

I don't even know why

I love you...

All you do is mope around,

I can't even look at you

You're so fat; I can't stand to touch you,

I can't talk to you; you haven't got anything

to say…………

Going home to meet the Sister

I had been with Stuart for six months when he decided that I should meet his sister Amanda; he didn't tell me until we were in the car that this could be a tricky meeting. Amanda had always got on well with his ex-wife Sue, so they had stayed in regular contact for the sake of their children.

Stuart thought that Amanda had probably sided with Sue, as he and Amanda hadn't ever really got on with each other, with an advanced form of sibling rivalry existing between them ever since his dad had married her mum when they were six and ten respectively. Plus, he hadn't spoken to her for a few months until he called to say we were visiting.

Hearing all this I did wonder why I was being taken halfway across the country to meet her, but this was answered with the plaintive 'don't you want to meet my sister?' What could I possibly say?

Like a lot of couples, it was the wife who had organised their social meetups, so Stuart hadn't been to see Amanda and her husband on his own for over ten years, but he assured me it would be fine.

Again, I wonder why I have agreed to this, only to say that if I had refused to meet her, it would have led to a marginally more uncomfortable situation.

Stuart also reveals now that he thinks he forgot to tell Amanda the things I don't eat, but Stuart says she won't be making anything like that, she said she is cooking a roast. What are the chances she would make a roast dinner with olives and tomatoes?

When we arrived the two nieces run and hide as soon as they see me, the five year old shouts from under the table to ask where Auntie Sue is, Stuart says she is polishing her cauldron, which goes over the five year old's head, and earns a black look from Amanda.

I stand awkwardly not knowing quite what to do, then Mike her husband appears and grabs the five year old from under the table and shoves her at me, 'say hello to Ellie you little monster' he chuckles, and with that the metaphorical life line reaches me.

Mike and I chat about work, telly, property prices, you know, all the grown-up stuff, while Amanda finishes off cooking dinner, and Stuart sulks in the garden smoking.

When it is time to eat the three year old is plonked in her highchair next to me where she spreads baked beans and fish fingers across her tray and over her face. I try not to notice the carnage, and the smell, which seems to indicate that she has been busy making use of the time until her dinner arrived, and a trip to the bathroom might have been a good idea.

Amanda carries one serving bowl out of the kitchen at a time, so that the green beans have been on the table a good ten minutes by the time the potatoes and casserole dish reach the table.

I couldn't swear to it, but it looks like she is taking pigeon steps until anyone notices her then she speeds up to elderly tortoise pace.

Whatever the food I pray it won't be cold, it definitely won't be hot, lukewarm food is my absolute pet hate, ok I am fussy, that isn't a crime. I am sure the dishes must be hot, so as long as I dig down, the food will still be warm enough, even for me. Also, this is evidently not shaping up to be a roast; the lid comes off the pot to reveal a slightly congealed Provençal chicken, 'don't worry if you touch the bowls' says Amanda 'they aren't hot'.

We tuck into all the foods I hate at the temperature I loathe, not quite cold but not warm, so approximately armpit temperature. I brace myself for a challenge.

Fortunately, we are able to serve ourselves, so I aim for the smallest piece of chicken from the bottom of the pot, and top up with potatoes. I nibble and push food around my plate while trying to engage in enough conversation so that no-one notices I am not eating much.

Finally, the main course is over, 'that was lovely' I lie, 'can I help you clear the table?' Amanda demurs so I stay where I am, the plates go out a sight quicker than they came in. Dessert is announced; it is Cheesecake - 'not homemade it is just out of a packet I'm afraid'. My horror is disguised by the big smile I plaster on my face, 'yum! But just a small slice for me' I say, 'it looks super rich' then for only the third time in my life I wade through a slice of vanilla cheesecake. With the consistency of rubberised washing up sponge, this could be a task in the vomit zone of the Crystal Maze.

Following coffee and some awkward conversation, Amanda talks incessantly about Stuart's daughters - how beautiful, sporty, musical and intelligent they are, how like their mother. There really isn't anything I can say, so I just smile to try and look like I am agreeing.

The three year old, while trying to get herself comfortable on the sofa, manages to kick me in the head; apart from a surprised 'Oof' I don't really react as neither parent nor Stuart makes any comment on my head injury. Then thank the good Lord above it is time to leave.

'That didn't go as badly as I expected' says Stuart, and it is this that leads to the best part of the evening, as I laugh so much that I need to go to the toilet in a layby - although by that point it could well have been hysteria.

The Ideal World Relationship Charter aka
The Equal Partnership

Having kissed so many frogs over the years, none of whom ever turned into a prince, a duke, a lord, a baron, or even a decent bloke, I decided that I had made all the mistakes I was prepared to make. At thirty-five it definitely felt past time to call in expert help; you know, so that I could have a relationship that works.

And what do you do in that situation? Why, break out the self-help books of course: 'He's just not that into you', 'Men are from Mars, Women are from Venus', 'Are you the one for me?' 'Better Relationships'.

It seems that the general thread of advice is to be mutually respectful, honest and open and have your own shite sorted out so that you can be the best version of yourself when you meet the other person. Now, realising that waiting until all my stuff was completely sorted to meet Mr Right, essentially meant that there would be no Mr Right. I decided I was rounded enough – I am impatient, short-tempered, and I won't share food, but that's ok because I know I am impatient, short-tempered and won't share food.....

So, the self-help books told me what healthy relationships were supposed to look like – mutual respect would allow us both to have our own beliefs and ideas without feeling the need to change each other.

Confidence in ourselves and each other would enable us to follow our independent interests without feeling threatened or jealous, and honesty would mean we both knew how each other was feeling.

Excellent communication would help us to tell each other and have discussions rather than rows. They also explained how to achieve these things, which I cannot go into here, you'll have to put the time in and read them yourself!

Armed with this information you might think I would have stopped making rookie mistakes, but then came along Mr Tim Perfect (as in Think I'M), and I made some of them all over again.

Number One: if he is sure you have met, and have been giving him the come on, and you cannot remember ever having seen him, so definitely couldn't have been giving him anything, don't go out with him as he has you confused with someone else. The fact he has the confidence to assure you of behaviour that isn't yours shows he is delusional.

Number Two: if when out to dinner he talks about things he 'knows' about you that are wrong, that are his assumptions or hearsay, say thank you for the meal and leave after the main course. Number Three: if he says 'I prefer conventionally pretty women, but there was something about you...' just leave.

Number Four: if he says 'you want someone who thinks you are the best thing since sliced bread and that isn't me', take him at his word and leave.

Number Five: if you spend the night together and he says 'hmm that wasn't as good as I thought it would be' consider saying 'oh, that's funny, you were as bad as I feared'. Then leave the room and never go back; if necessary move house, car and name, but definitely block his phone number and never speak to him again, let alone let him back into your bed-chamber.

Number Six: when he tells you that he has been divorced for six months, and you find out that they didn't file the divorce papers until just before you met, and he was still sharing a bedroom with his ex, expect everything else to be lies too.

Number Seven: when he lets his kids tell you to drop dead, jump on your furniture in their shoes, and break your possessions without correcting them, then says in front of them that you shouldn't be so horrible to the little darlings, open the front door and ask them all to leave, even if it is raining, snowing or there is a tornado.

I do not blame Tim for our time together; I blame myself for seeing him; he was an arse from day one, and that never changed. I just let my friends convince me that he was a good bloke and so ignored my instincts and let people tell me he was a good catch - DON'T DO THIS!

It seemed that I needed a more organised Plan of Action, so after we parted I formulated the 'Ideal

World Relationship Charter to enable space for personal growth' otherwise known as 'The Equal Partnership'.

A simple go-to-guide to help me use all I had learnt; please feel free to borrow the Charter to help iron out any of your relationship woes.

We begin with the 'Statement of Intent', a bit business-like but it is important to lay out your expectations for the other person: 'each person is to take responsibility for their own personal growth, and shared responsibility for the growth of the relationship. Through talking, listening, having fun together and apart, by clearly, and honestly communicating what you want and what you have to offer'. Ok, so far so good, I mean that does make sense, right?

We both need to be responsible for sorting out our own baggage, and we accept joint responsibility for putting in the effort towards being a couple. Plus, there won't be any of that second-guessing to find out what we each want. Yes, that is all very mature I'd say.

Now on to the practical: 'Each person is to pay 50% of household bills and to do 50% of all household tasks'; again this seems very fair, aren't we are all equal in this day and age? What with everyone having choices, and jobs, our own money and whatnot.

So yes, let this home be an example of true equality, none of that 'I have done the vacuuming for you' - for me darling? How thoughtful, what? Aren't you shedding any hair or skin cells towards making the dust? Well, that is nice of you.

Hold on; I have learnt through bitter experience to double check the wording on documents... '50% of all household tasks', now that sounds specific, but what if the 100% of household tasks involved isn't the same for both people? Is making a shopping list and going out to buy the shopping included? Mowing the lawn? Choosing and buying birthday cards and presents? Booking holidays? Checking we are getting the best deal on utility bills? There is so much more to running a house than the washing up.

Underneath the common sense, there is an opportunity for war, so just in case someone doesn't understand what needs doing, I designed a list, of course I did.

Daily jobs include: tidy all rooms before bed, fold dry towels and put back on rails in the bathroom, clean bath, shower and sink, sweep all floors, put cups into the dishwasher, replace magazines in the rack, straighten cushions, put bottles into recycling, put each remote control with their appliance.

Wash up (reload and unload the dishwasher) and put clean things back into cupboards, disinfect worktops and splashbacks in kitchen, water houseplants. Make the bed, choose and make dinner, put the rubbish in bin or compost, and feed the animals.

Cat and Flick to be fed half a tin each on the green table on the patio; Arnie is to be asked to sit and wait before he is allowed his food, which he doesn't like cold from the fridge, so needs to be warmed in the microwave for 10 seconds.

Top up their water bowls from a pre-boiled and cooled down kettle, change the cat litter tray, pick up poo in the garden, walk Arnie – no sticks. Water the garden if necessary.

Weekly jobs include: Dusting – ceiling to floor - this is the better way round so that as the dust floats down, the lower level dusting picks it up. Vacuum –

including under and behind furniture; empty household bins into the appropriate area – black, recycling, glass - clean bathroom including tiles, toilet inside and out, top up toilet rolls.

Clean the kitchen cupboards in and outside, tiles, microwave in and out, oven inside and out, fridge inside and out, dust top of cabinets and fan behind the refrigerator. Check salt and rinse aid levels in the dishwasher, empty tray in the bottom of the washing machine. Put washing on, and then out to dry, into the airing cupboard, iron, and back into wardrobes.

Mop all hard floors, don't forget to go under and behind furniture, change the bedclothes – try to co-ordinate pillowcases to the duvet and bottom sheet. Make a shopping list, buy and unpack shopping, mow the lawn, put wheelie bins out.

Monthly jobs are: Clean all windows inside and out including frames and sills, flea and worming treatments for Cat, Flick and Arnie, and dust air vents.

Yearly tasks include: Trimming the hedges, booking Cat, Flick and Arnie's boost jabs, take above to vet appointment. Organise pet insurance quotes to make sure have the best deal, organise car insurance quotes.

Get car tax, book car in for a service, take the car for service, book MOT, take the car for MOT. Organise house insurance quotes. Gift and card shopping for birthdays, Christmas, Easter, Mother's day, Father's day, Anniversaries.

Wrapping and delivering said gifts, writing cards and posting. Booking holiday, organising pet-sitter for Cat, Flick and Arnie, making sure paperwork is up to date for travelling including insurance, packing cases.

Ad hoc jobs such as buying, writing and sending Get Well cards, speaking to organisations regarding bills, repairs etc, waiting in when necessary, and finally, any DIY tasks as needed.

Blimey, reading it back I think that the house should be immaculate, that is so organised I have impressed myself.

However, trying to see it from a bloke's point of view it does sound a bit control freak having it all listed out like that, they might not get that it's supposed to reduce stress and possible arguments.

A man might well think that's not the sort of woman he would want to share a house with. Do I sound like that to other people? Bugger! that's probably what people have meant when they have told me to chill out.

Also, I think that I may have inadvertently forgotten one of the main biological differences between men and women, understanding the purpose of cushions: for women they are an accessory to finish a room, something to lean on or cuddle.

Men, on the other hand, don't 'get' cushions, they think nothing of throwing your good cushions on the floor; folding them in half under their heads so they can see the telly better or even to rest… their… feet… on; Believe me, I have seen them do it.

Asking a straight man to straighten a cushion? They wouldn't fluff them up or put them at jaunty angles – the most you can expect is that they will be lined up like soldiers.

I am already shaking my head at myself in a disappointed 'ahh you poor thing' kind of way. I wrote this, and even I think a prospective life partner would have to be very keen to get any further than point two.

On to item three of the charter, yes that's all we've got up to, each person to organise and take the other out on a date once a month; now that's better, not an unreasonable request at all, a little romance never hurt anyone.

Item four: to go out once a month on a mutually arranged outing, again that's absolutely fine. Item five: To find a shared interest that we chose together, to build shared friendships; ok, slightly Howard and Hilda, but not that bad (look it up, 'Ever Decreasing Circles', never have matching anoraks been so entertaining).

Item Six: To have a separate interest which we do alone or with friends; how very sensible, and healthy, maintain your independence and have confidence that you can be apart and it doesn't threaten the relationship. Note: this interest should not be drugs, alcohol, sex, porn or gambling.

Item Seven: We should not have to ask each other if we can do something, out of courtesy when making a plan we should make the other aware. Therefore, suggest each should keep a diary so that any individual plans we make do not encroach on our quality time as a couple.

Ok, I can kind of see where I was going with this, but keeping a diary was just that step too far, it is all efficient but who really fancies making plans by this point? Unless they involve packing your belongings into your car when I am out doing one of my separate interests and moving without leaving a forwarding address.

Item Eight: To be able to ask each other for reassurance and receive it, when it is needed. It sounds a bit more normal until you overthink the last part - when it is needed? It could be a time you cannot give it, 'I need you to hold me....' 'Umm... I am just having a poo - can it wait?...' 'no, I desperately need a hug' or vice versa.

What if you disagree with what they want reassurance for? 'I want to tell my mother I have never forgiven her for giving my eagle eyes action man to the jumble, and that's why I have decided to put her in the worst rated care home I can find'? 'I want to tell my boss that he can shove his job, I have always wanted to be a hair model'.

If he is under the car in the middle of an oil change and you need to talk about your fear of growing old, does he come out and let the oil drain into the water table, or do you climb under? You see it all gets very complicated.

Item Nine: To listen to each other's point of view when there are disagreements and to let the other person know that, although we do not agree, we do want to understand their point of view and that they are entitled to their feelings so that both people can feel heard and not discounted.

I must have been reading a Relate book when I wrote this, just to clarify whether you say all this before or after throwing plates and stuff? Item Ten: Cook together or to take turns cooking for each other. I was beginning to think I had gone over the edge and then it goes back to being sane again.

Item Eleven: To appreciate that our lives, pressures and disappointments may be different, but both are of equal value. Sure, yeah, no, yes, of course, that could be a tricky one to live out if one of you is a brain surgeon, and the other one is a jewellery designer.

I mean no-one actually died from not having precisely the right necklace to go with that deep navy plunge neck, mid length, cocktail dress, unless of course, you know different.

Item Twelve: To make a point of appreciating what we do for each other by saying please and thank you, although there is nothing wrong with this point there does seem to have been some amnesia around a particular person that proves someone can have beautiful manners and still be a dickhead.

If you can get past all that and think that the Charter is a good idea, there is another practical point to ponder: when is the best time to present the Relationship Charter to a partner, or potential partner?

I mean you definitely wouldn't want to offer it at any point during the first date. 'So Margo, tell me about yourself...'

'Well, Giles, just before we get into that can I show you the Relationship Charter that I and therefore any future partner of mine needs to abide by...' err... no.

Or 'Oh Margo your skin is so soft, it makes me want to...'

'Hmm Giles, that feels so good...but just before we get going, so to speak, can I get you to read through this...'

It seems unfair to wait until he likes you and more importantly thinks you are perfectly 'normal' to land this on him. That's a bit 'Crying Game' for me 'SURPRISE!' Ok, so it's a metaphorical willy rather than an actual willy, but you know what I mean.

Maybe with internet dating, this is less of a problem than I am making it; instead of bothering to write a witty or alluring profile, or get your friend to describe you impartially (Thanks Dee by the way), you could use the charter, with a sign off something like 'sign the charter and let's talk, who knows I could be your true love'.

Going home to meet the parents – Chas

When we arrived at his parent's house I waited at the gate while he rang the front doorbell, we couldn't just drive on to the property, Chas said, they wouldn't like that.

The parents were cordial to him and slightly less than warm to me, and I noticed straight away there was no hugs or kisses for the son they hadn't seen in six months. Before I could even get out of the car, there were clear instructions about where on the property I could park, and which direction the car should face.

I could feel my rebellious spirit starting to struggle, can I turn it around later after stretching my legs? No, because they didn't want the exhaust to be directed towards the vegetable patch. As I turned the car, they stood to watch me, arms folded, Mr giving instructions when he felt I wasn't giving an optimal turning performance.

Once out of the car I was told I could call them Mr and Mrs Tity (names changed for entertainment purposes). We went inside and sat around the kitchen table, despite our two hour journey the kettle was not put on, and no other liquid refreshment was offered.

It transpired over the course of the visit that Chas had descended from camels; there were three cups of tea taken per day, one at breakfast, one at lunch and dinner. No other drinks would be provided outside of these times unless there was an emergency (which I guess did not include dehydration), when you could have a glass of tap water.

After a while of awkward questions aimed at their son 'How are you getting on with the mortgage?', 'have you been offered promotion?', they both showed us upstairs to our room; we were in the same room but had twin beds with a cupboard between. We were told that 'we don't expect anything to go on' in their house, and they showed us where we could put our bags, 'on the floor, definitely not on the bedcovers or chairs'.

Next was the shower room, we were fortunate to have a room with an en-suite; after talking me through the furniture in the room Mr Tity told me he would explain the instructions for the shower. I assumed that the instructions would tell me about temperamental fittings, but they did, in fact, tell me exactly how to shower in their home.

The instructions were actually typed, laminated and fixed to the wall next to the cubicle: 1. Do not run the shower before getting under the water 2. Stand under the flow for maximum of 30 seconds 3. Turn the water off, apply soap and shampoo 4. After washing there is a further 90 seconds allowed to have the water back on to rinse.

And no, this was not a joke, this was water conservation at its most militant. The toilet in this bathroom was 'for urination only, if you wish to defecate there is a bathroom downstairs for that'.

After the parents were satisfied that I understood the rules and agreed to abide by them, they went downstairs leaving the bedroom door open (no sneaky kissing in this house). I whispered my hilarity over the military operation that had been our arrival, but Chas was not joining in (through fear of hidden cameras I think).

Asking what would happen if I broke the rules, Chas looked stricken as he told me about an incident with a previous girlfriend he had brought home who suffered from OCD. The poor girl needed three showers a day, which had resulted in Mr Tity banging on the en-suite door telling her she had used too much water and that she had to come out of the bathroom immediately, and he would wait there until she did. I can only wonder why that relationship came to an end.

Back downstairs we were offered a tour of Mr Tity's campsite, which was plainly his pride and joy. We spent nearly two hours with him explaining the quality of the hedging plants, why that variety had been chosen, where they were bought and how much they cost, how long they would take to mature, what the bushes would look like as they grew, how the new toilet block had been designed, what had been done to the drainage system to accommodate this new arrangement, and how much it had cost.

He detailed the superiority of the site as a whole, mainly because of his rigorous attention to detail, which included each caravan, (no tents thank you), being allowed two days on a spot before he would come and tell the guest to move to the adjoining plot so that his grass wouldn't be damaged by their vehicle.

It must have made for a relaxing week's holiday to keep taking down the awning, packing away all their stuff and moving the caravan to the next pitch along to accommodate the welfare of the grass.

On the second day we were allowed to see inside their motor home, where we approached it quietly so as not to disturb some nesting swallows. No, Mr and Mrs Tity hadn't actually been anywhere in the motorhome, due to its sheer size it was impractical for driving on country lanes, but Mrs Tity did enjoy quietly sitting in it with her knitting from time to time.

On reflection, my joke about lending it to us so we could take the dogs on holiday was probably ill-judged.

By the evening of the second day dehydration and military procedures were pushing me to my tolerance limit, and what I really needed to calm myself was a proper bath, three cups of coffee one after the other, and a massive bar of fruit and nut. With none of these an option, I stared out of the window at the empty campsite and wished the clock to move faster.

Every family has its eccentricities, but this was seriously uncomfortable, not only was this plainly an emotionally unhealthy family under the control of a megalomaniac, but it was one that I would not want to be a part of and have to mix with at every significant holiday or event for the rest of my life.

Like the OCD woman before me, I knew this relationship would have to end, so I smiled and

made polite noises through the next 12 hours before
I could leave and break their son's heart.

Going to meet the (Upper Middle Class) parents – Shea

Shea's reputation as a character, always up to mischief and general silliness, usually the first person to suggest fancy dress or a practical joke, went before him - so I thought he would be annoying and impossible to have a proper conversation with.

I was wrong - he was funny, and he was also sensitive, with his confidence faltering ever so slightly in the most endearing way. We were different people really, but it seemed to work for us both, and it wasn't long before Shea had asked me to come with him on his next visit home.

He said his mum, in particular, was keen to meet me, as his first 'proper' girlfriend, this didn't mean his first nudge, nudge, wink, wink 'proper', but the first one he had actually mentioned to them.

Shea had talked to me for hours about the town where he grew up, his circle of friends and the things they got up to: the little school, the woods where he played as a child; he had said his dad was strict, his mum not, and that his sister was absolutely fantastic, so I felt prepared, and not at all nervous about meeting them.

As they lived at the other end of the country, we decided to have a holiday most of the way there, and then go on to visit.

We spent three idyllic days at a gorgeous country hotel - the sort of place where you can forget the rest of the world in lovely, romantic, frisky days. We slept late, walked hand in hand through meadows, picnicked under trees, gazed into each other's eyes over late dinners, and did all the things you imagine you might do on your first mini-break.

On the third day Shea was up, showered and dressed by the time I woke up, he handed me a coffee, and told me to get up, as apparently there were only two hours left to have breakfast, shower, get ready, and pack before we had to go; we could not in any circumstances be late.

As a 'leave it until the last minute person' I couldn't really see the rush, but dragged myself up and spent longer preening than I usually would for a full night out. It did start a twinge of anxiety that my chilled out man seemed to be getting stressed, I had never seen this side of him and it threw me a bit.

With my hair beaten into submission I started looking for something to wear, I was advised not to pick anything too short, too brash or that showed my tattoo (the word 'family' in a small circle), a tricky instruction as Shea knew well that my clothing options were short, low cut, or both.

Apparently, his dad had been a parole officer in years past and still believed tattoos belonged to inmates, so I would have to wear a cardigan and remember not to take it off. His mum was a social worker and was old school enough to still believe that showing a bit of leg and cleavage made you a likely candidate for her services. (She actually kept a tin of beans and a cheap loaf of bread in her desk in case one of her clients came in bemoaning their lack of money to buy food for themselves and their children).

After choosing what we hoped was my least offensive outfit we headed out.

On the way there more subtle signs of stress developed - creasing of the brow, the shoulders getting closer to the ears - that sort of thing; we went through a car wash in the services, and threw away all the rubbish we had accumulated in the footwells.

We pulled into a 'nice' road with quite a prominent sign saying 'PRIVATE'. Shea shook his head, 'Dad said he was going to put a bigger sign up to stop people who don't live here driving down the road.' Oh bugger! now this could get very messy - council estate meets private estate. I took a deep breath to try and steady my pounding heart.

We pulled on to the drive in front of a very nice house, it wasn't a mansion, but it was much too large for two people. As Shea let us in it was clear no-one was home, and we both relaxed a little.

Dropping our bags in the hallway we did a quick tour of living room, dining room, kitchen, music room (yes, it really was a whole room just for playing instruments and listening to music), the butterflies in my stomach ramped up preparations for take-off.

I can only imagine Shea had thoughtfully decided to take my mind off my nerves as he pulled me up the stairs, it became crystal clear he had decided to throw caution to the wind and christen his old bedroom.

I was against the idea, what if his parents came back? But he assured me that they had left a message and they were still in town, which was a good twenty minutes away, plenty of time for some speedy action.

I allowed myself to be persuaded, at that stage in our relationship any free moment could be gainfully employed 'exploring intimate connections'... ahem.

Once in full flow, everything else was of course forgotten, but during some vocal encouragement on my behalf the front door slammed and Shea's dad bellowed 'Hello Shea, I am back now'. He had plainly heard the whole thing.

and napkin, and the whole lot on a tray covered with a crisp white cloth.

I stared at the arrangement for a minute or two trying to decide how on earth to start, they nearly died of shock when I picked up the apple and took a large bite.

As he yanked on his jeans and straightened his hair Shea tried to convince me that it was okay, we hadn't been caught, his Dad always made an entrance, but even after our hurried dressing and tidying ourselves up we came down to a crimson blush that told another story.

Having to meet a prospective father-in-law knowing they have just heard you having really loud and a bit rude sex with their son is a hard thing to carry off with dignity.

Fortunately, things picked up from there, and a lovely visit was had, I think, by all. There were one or two cultural differences that we had to bridge.

My Brummie accent confused them, and I had to repeat myself more than once or twice, and when they offered me some fruit after lunch, I really wasn't expecting that apple to arrive on a plate with knife

An Older Sister's Advice

Dear Kat,

You know not to drink red wine because you feel angry or upset; it leads to more silly disagreements that only make you feel much worse! Everything gets more emotional than it needs to be, so if you do need to argue then at least do it with a clear head, you poor thing.

It does sound awful from how you describe it, and if Niall decides not to continue with your relationship, I know how upsetting and painful it will be for you both. I know how sure you feel that you and Niall are 'right' for each other and that you thought that this could go the distance.

Unlike some of your past beaux you two do seem to share the same values, and your life experiences, although different, have produced similar effects, you just seem to recognise each other. However, darling, if this is going to end, you need to try to remember that Niall has his own emotional issues, and they will have affected his decision. Before you he had been single for so long that he probably isn't yet fully used to having to think about anyone else's feelings.

You know that he is scared of not being good enough for you as he is and, equally, as frightened of the changes he might have to make to his life to be a better partner - not that you have asked him to change, I know.

You know the challenge of cutting down on alcohol consumption, it is a real addiction, and that won't be made any easier if Niall isn't comfortable to accept any help; socially acceptable or not, alcohol is a drug and one that you can hide behind for many years.

It is likely to be a tough time for him (and you). I do feel for Niall, being a people pleaser avoids having to deal with confrontation, but it also covers up his true feelings, much harder to do with a clear head. That is a lot for someone to consider doing, and that is without all the usual stuff that people compromise on and niggle over in relationships.

If Niall has not been able to do these things for himself for whatever reason, then think how tricky he would find it to be in any healthy relationship.

In a relationship with you, that struggle would inevitably end up having a negative impact on your wellbeing. Pushing your buttons, even though you are good enough, you have not done something wrong, and you are very lovable.

I only say this because I worry about your health, and, am fully aware that you have no intention of having another episode and ending up in hospital.

You may not like thinking about it, but it is important, to be honest with yourself about the possible pitfalls in this relationship.

Whatever decision Niall makes it does not change the fact that during your time together you have opened up to a potential partner and been very honest, that has been harder for you than you would have thought, but it has definitely been worth it.

You love someone who genuinely loves you in return, who is intelligent enough to be able to discuss things without flying off the deep end and admit when they are wrong, who has given you the space to sort yourself out and not tried to control what you do or how you do it.

Even if it ends between you, at least you have some wonderful memories.

I know that there is a little part of you who is scared that you are going to be abandoned, as your first and overriding reaction after the argument, the thought of losing Niall, was excruciating and felt like it would be the end of the world.

However, now you have had a chance to think it through, I hope that you are reassured that you will always have me.

No matter who else may be in your life! and hopefully if you keep reminding yourself that you do not have any firm answers yet and that you need to be able to think clearly about looking after yourself, it will be a little easier.

Although this argument has left you both shaken it may just be part of finding your feet - it is a new and intense relationship and unfortunately comes with more than its share of baggage on both sides.

Please do keep in touch, come and stay whenever you can, the children miss their Auntie KitKat.

I hope that helps, even a bit, lots of love forever and ever gorgeous girl.

from your Big Sis kiss kiss.

Poem For You

Strong pair of arms whose strength to lean back into,

The soft loving eyes I gaze into,

Seeing me the way I want to be seen.

Curved body behind mine as I sleep

keeping me safe from bad dreams, bad things,

Large brown hands keeping the connection with

mine when out in the world

Safe and sound, loved and respected,

appreciated and wanted,

All I ever wanted,

never thought I would have,

but now all is mine.

The reason why I don't eat pork chops

The first time a boyfriend offered to cook me a romantic dinner I said yes without taking it as a proper invitation, meaning that I had already had my sausage and mash when I received the call to ask if I was still coming over as I was late.

Not remembering anything about the arrangement I was caught off guard, so fibbed and said 'of course, I am just on my way'.

When I arrived his mum and dad were in the lounge watching Saturday night telly, but they assured me they wouldn't gate-crash our dinner, the dining room table was set beautifully with red roses and candles as a centrepiece. I was impressed, and then felt guilty and undeserving that I hadn't even remembered.

James served a melon starter, complete with glacé cherry topper, and sparkling white wine. As a seventeen year old I hadn't really got the hang of alcohol just yet and was pleasantly fuzzy by the time the main course arrived. A massive plate of pork chops, roast potatoes, and more vegetables than my family would serve in a week was put in front of me.

I had no idea how I was going to be able to eat even half of this with my already full stomach. I need not have worried. Fate had already decreed that I would not have to worry about food for too much longer that night, and for the coming weeks.

James suggested that we link arms over the table to drink our wine, but as he leaned in his sleeve lightly brushed the candle flame, and changed his life forever. He leapt up in horror as the orange flame licked around his elbow, and his shirt began to dissolve.

I froze, unable to comprehend what I was seeing, and had no idea how to help at all. His screams brought his mum running; fortunately, she had been a St John's Ambulance volunteer, and her training kicked in. Pushing James to the kitchen sink, she turned both taps on full, with water cascaded over his arm the fire was turned into steam and smoke in seconds.

James' screams and cries filled our ears over the running water, his dad stood beside me, visibly shaken, while his mum tried to soothe James with her own voice shaky with tears. We laid him down on the floor next to a large bowl so that he could keep his arm underwater as he fainted from the pain and shock.

We all stayed up all night taking turns to bring a new bowl of water every fifteen minutes. His arm looked horrific, with skin dissolved, and burns into the muscles of his arm. The next morning was a Sunday, so James' parents made him an emergency doctor's appointment.

The on-rota GP must have had the shock of his life when a lad stumbled in with his arm open, yellow and gory being protected from the world by a damp tea towel. The shaken doctor sent him straight to the accident and emergency unit next door with a referral to the burns specialist team.

Over the next three months, I visited James in the burns centre, sitting with him while his dressings were changed, neither of us saying much. We were both too young, too traumatised and without emotional support to help us to know what on earth to say to each other.

I was there the day he came home, pale and skinny, with his arm in a huge bandage. His mum took me to one side and asked that as she had to go back to work, I visit him during the day to make sure he wasn't sitting in on his own all the time.

By now an understandable depression had slid over him, and James much preferred to spend his days in bed staring at the wall. Still, I sat with him, mainly silent and unable to even think of what to say beyond the silly gossip of friends he had lost touch with months ago; as long as I sat there, he wasn't alone.

Eventually, even the outpatient treatments came to an end, and a week after his final skin graft, James broke up with me. I didn't blame him, I belonged to a dark part of his life that he would much rather forget. I tried to put it all behind me, and just about did, but every time my mum cooked pork chops the smell made my heart stop.

Afterwards

Mickey has moved out, I couldn't wait for him to leave in the end, all the shouting, the moods, the confusion, that sick upside down unsettled feeling in my stomach all the time.

I wanted to get my space back, now in the quiet, I think, what if the problem was me? Does that mean that I am doomed to be on my own? With only my parents for company, and all alone when they inevitably die.

I have scary thoughts that everyone is happier without me; Mickey and his kids are pleased, more chilled out by not being with me, he says they weren't ready for a Step mum. I ask why he didn't decide that before we got married; he can only shrug.

I invited myself to Patsy's candle party, it was nerve-wracking with all the people in and out, and I had to remind myself not to mention the split; sometimes I catch myself talking about it and think 'how did the conversation get here?' The other person wouldn't have asked whether I had a recent break-up, or when the last time I spoke to another person was.

If I carry on like this people will try to avoid me, maybe they are already, how would I know? After an hour and buying a box of Relaxation Votives, I make my excuses, I was tired anyway.

I only have two days to prepare myself for my 'Cake decorating for beginners' class, I am supposed to go back this Wednesday and am dreading it. Why do I put myself up for these things? Jackie said it's because I do want to do them, then when the time comes status quo bias makes it easier not to do it, so even though you want things to be different, it is easier for them to stay the same.

Having a psychology student as a friend can be very helpful in finding out what your mind is doing without you realising, but sometimes I think that is just another thing to be overwhelmed by. When it is too quiet at home, I might talk to Jackie and imagine what she would say to me, even though she isn't there, it makes me feel less alone.

Last night she urged me on to sort out the photographs, one pile for me, one for him, and one that might go in the bin, or back in the box to go up in the loft if I don't feel like parting with them. Jackie said it would help me feel connected to my friends, my family and my happy memories; and I thought that sounded like a better use of time than laying on the sofa staring at the television.

Popped into Mum's while she was at the day centre, cleaned her worktops and tided the bathroom, made sure the note telling her to put her leftovers in the bin was pinned to the fridge, and reminded her that making a pile next to the rubbish bin is almost right but doesn't work as well because then it makes a mess on the floor. I don't think the note will make any difference, it hasn't so far, but I keep trying to find a way to make it work better.

As I am closing the front door Mrs Thing from next door asks how she is today, 'much the same' I say, not sure what she expects me to say, mum isn't likely to be the first person to reverse the ageing process. She says something about the kids not seeing their Gran recently, I check my watch and say 'I've got to go' and walk away, I am not going to tell her all my private business.

Mickey text me to say that he feels relieved that we made a decision and that his new flat being near the kid's mum means that they can pop in when they want to, it is he says, 'more natural'. He doesn't ask how I am, or what I am doing, but does mention that if we bump into each other, we should have a coffee or something. I am not sure what to reply, so I don't for the time being.

Later, he texts to say the kids being able to pop in and out is what he has always wanted, and now if I would just pop in and shag him once in a while, then everything would be perfect.

Day out at the STI Clinic

My friend Caroline has led a very sheltered life and has only been with one man who she met at nineteen. She lives through, and for, the next instalment of her Celebrity magazines and soap operas.

But, more than celebrity and drama, Caroline finds sex fascinating; other people's sex to be precise. She is intrigued to find out what other people 'get up to'. She once confided to me that while cooking the nightly dinner she propped her laptop on the kitchen worktop so she could watch porn while getting the dinner done "just to educate myself".

I have tried telling her that porn is nothing like real life, but I don't think she believes me, and thinks that all single people spend their life bent in funny angles over desks / car bonnets / kitchen worktops etc.

having loud, messy orgasms. It isn't that she would want to have an affair, and I don't think she is planning to surprise Mr Caroline with some cheeky BDSM roleplay, more like she wishes that she had done a bit more 'dating' before settling down.

I tell you this so that it explains why Caroline thinks that going to be tested for a sexually transmitted disease will be fun. "Oh, can I come with you?" she says, and I can feel her holding her breath as if I have just offered her a spare ticket to the Caribbean or an all-expenses-paid shopping trip to Harrods.

I remind her that this visit is needed because I just found out that my last boyfriend was less than faithful, and I want to make sure that he hasn't left me any other nasty little surprises to be going on with. Now is the time to look after me, and that I'm a little bit scared to think about the possible outcome, 'of course, yes, you are right, how insensitive of me', she consoles.

Unfortunately, this contrition only lasts a minute because as soon as I say it would be nice to have someone come to keep me company she gets all carried away again, 'I hope there will be prostitutes there,' she claps her hands in gleeful anticipation...

When the day of the appointment arrives we have to climb five flights of stairs to get to the clinic (no lift is available, and I wonder don't they expect people in wheelchairs to need their services? Or are the stairs some subtle form of punishment to those of us having dodgy encounters? Or maybe they want to tire us out so that we don't have any energy left for sex).

The brightly lit reception area in tones of inoffensive beige with various pot plants and educational posters that remind visitors how important it is to share *all* the relevant information, and that you can get a free Chlamydia test by post if you are in your teens, is an immediate disappointment to Caroline. 'What did you expect?' I enquire shaking my head a little, 'a line of disapproving medical professionals, all tending to a queue of overly made-up women wearing leather mini-skirts, fishnet tights and stilettos with goldfish in the heels and men with greasy comb-overs?'

Caroline just shrugs and says 'it looks just like a waiting room', which of course is just what it is.

After taking my name, the receptionist hands me a clipboard; the questions begin reasonably safely: have you had sex? (Would I be here if I hadn't?) But they soon enter territory usually only reserved for close friends, what sorts of sex have you had?

Oral? Anal? Same-sex partners? Had a tattoo abroad? Used intravenous drugs? Shared needles? Have you had sex for money? Or do you work in the sex industry? Have you had partners without using barrier forms of contraception? Do you have any symptoms? How long since your last sexual health check-up? Phew.

Clearly disappointed with the other people in the waiting room, (a clean-cut woman in her early twenties reading a handbag sized Cosmo, and a dishevelled man in his late sixties staring into the middle distance) Caroline makes her own entertainment 'Go on, say you are a sex worker, let's see what they do' she encourages. 'I can't help feeling you are not taking this very seriously' I say quietly, 'and I don't think they will do anything other than stick swabs in my every orifice and give me a carrier bag of free condoms'.

Unsurprisingly I refuse to pretend to be a sex worker, and with all questions answered the clipboard goes back to the receptionist. After a much longer wait than you would expect with only three people waiting, a doctor calls my name and leads Caroline and me through a security door into a side office.

The doctor looks quizzically at Caroline - 'I need my friend to be with me' I say, and manage not to say 'this poor woman needs this experience just as much as I do, but for different reasons, so come on let's inject some excitement into her life'.

The doctor doesn't introduce himself which I find a bit rude considering he is about to know more about me than my own family, and how much of me he is going to get to see. Therefore, using all my creative capabilities, I will call him 'Dr No Name'.

'So...' he fidgets as he glances over my answers and then, unnecessarily I think, asks me the questions all over again. I answer them truthfully, he nods with each one but does not comment.

At a previous clinic I went to many years ago after a similar boyfriend debacle, a rotund middle-aged nurse with a massive smile and the tightest curly perm known to womankind, listened to my answers and then gave me a long good-natured lecture about respecting my body and myself, and the dangers of unprotected sex.

I guess in the intervening years the focus has changed from 'look, just do what we tell you', into 'we won't tell you what you should do, everyone can do what they want, and no-one is allowed to judge' – professionally at any rate.

'Is there anything I haven't mentioned?' Dr No Name asks tentatively, I look him straight in the eye and say 'Anal, you didn't ask about anal'. He is flustered by this, looking at the paperwork, the screen, back to the paperwork – anywhere but directly at me.

He is so uncomfortable, which I would not expect for someone who works here, that I almost want to say 'it's ok, don't worry about this other stuff, I only came in with a sore big toe, would you rather think about that?' But I don't. 'Ah no, ok......' he pauses and lets the unasked question hang in the air so that he doesn't have to say the word - 'No' I say, 'no anal'.

Now that is over we three traipse to the next room, the one with the bed and the stirrups, which I cannot see the point of as I am quite capable of opening my legs and keeping them open, as being here has proven.

On pulling down my pants, I realised just how long it has been since my last wax, and feel the need to quietly apologise to Caroline about the unkempt nature of my down below. I just know that she is the sort of person who would never miss a waxing appointment because someone offered her coffee and cake and the times clashed, so will be perfectly coiffured in all areas at all times.

I do wonder briefly how close friendship should get, but it is far too late to worry about that now that I am trapped here with my lady area catching the breeze, well it would have been if there had been one.

At this point a second doctor comes in and introduces herself, she is here to supervise Dr No

Name; it doesn't occur to me at the time to ask why he needs supervision. Sitting on the little stool between my legs he looks like he is about to have a coronary.

I have the urge to announce gladiator style 'Let the examination begin!' but I don't want him to have unduly shaky hands for the next part.

Without a word he begins, and after quite a few minutes of poking and fiddling around, accompanied by the scraping noise of instruments being opened and closed, he puts down the instruments and *pushes his little stool on wheels backwards and disappears through the curtains*.

That impresses me, because that is just the sort of thing I would like to do – not a gynaecological examination, but finish a meeting by pushing off on my chair on wheels and disappearing backwards through curtains, without saying a word - now that's what you call an exit.

Having wriggled out of the stirrups, I am just getting back into my pants when we hear Dr Two say quietly 'Umm.....I still don't feel completely confident that you can recognise the difference between the urethral and vaginal openings'.
Caroline and I turned to stare at each other, eyes and mouths wide open, stunned and horrified, we dissolved into breath stealing giggles. Somehow, I don't wet myself, although it's a close-run thing.

Despite what has gone before the next bit is where there could be a real problem - it is blood test time. I explain to Dr No Name about my needle phobia and that I will probably cry, which he can ignore; but there is a good chance that I will pass out so if I could lay down this will probably be better.

He says nothing but points to the chair that is waiting for all the non-phobic people, he rests my arm on a pillow and gets fiddling about on his table. Instantly queasy I look at the wall trying to make sure I don't see anything needle-like and begin chattering in Caroline's direction to try and distract myself while he starts stabbing me with the needle.
After several minutes I am just blacking out when he stops; I manage to say 'oh thank God that's over', and just as I lose consciousness he says 'I haven't been able to do it yet, I cannot find a vein'.

I come to with something unusual happening, the usually mild-mannered Caroline is quietly shrieking (no, I didn't think that was possible either) at Dr No Name 'you've been stabbing around for 5 minutes, my friend has passed out, and now you say you haven't even done it yet?' He shrugs and backs out of the room.

When he goes I begin to crawl out of the chair, 'that's good I can leave now, he isn't coming back' I say. However, now her dander is up, Caroline isn't wasting any of it, locking me with a steely stare she practically orders me to stay where I am. Once back in position her tone changes back to the soft one that she normally uses with me; she tells me that Dr No Name will be back in just a minute and then it will all be over.

Wouldn't it be a shame after all we have been through if we went home now - I am tempted to say 'it isn't we, it's me,' but I don't. Dr No Name comes back in and prepares to try again, but Caroline won't let him near me unless he promises to use a baby-sized needle and he only gets one try. I have never seen her more Amazonian, and as Dr No Name apparently doesn't want to risk what Caroline will do to him if he screws up this time, he very carefully takes my blood, and although I am momentarily relieved, I still pass out again.

Before we even make it back down the five flights of stairs and into the fresh air we have exploded into fits of laughter - 'I am not sure you know which hole is which? Hello? He probably doesn't even belong in this department if he doesn't know that!'
Which led to speculation on where he really came from, we speculated on what Dr No Name's real job might have been - as a bus driver? gardener? man who usually works behind the coffee bar near A&E? which gives us hysterics.

Between snorts, I managed to say 'I think I know what it was, it's June, it must be work experience week, mine must be the first hoo-ha he has ever seen judging by how scared he was, poor bugger'.

Every time we manage to stop laughing something sets us off again, given that he said so little I wonder aloud whether he may have been a Trappist monk.

For months afterwards we can dissolve into laughter with just the merest mention of work experience or doctors, each setting off the other with our comments 'at least it won't be such a shock on his wedding night', 'I wonder if he has had to have therapy?' 'I wonder if he reliably knows one hole from the other yet?' 'Did he go back to driving a bus the next day do you reckon?'

Despite being sworn to secrecy, Caroline confessed that she hadn't been able to contain herself, and only lasted a few days before she caved in and told her husband, Tim, all about it.

Tim was very shocked - I suspect he assumed that we spent our time together in benign ways, going shopping or drinking coffee and that our conversations revolved around knitting patterns and recipes. He did not think it was funny, in fact, he was horrified, and I lost the last of my brownie points.

Imagine my taking his 'virgin' bride (yeah, maybe she was twenty years ago mate - check her browser) to such a place, my misbehaviour sullied her, I was guilty in his eyes even though it was The Plonker who had cheated on me.

In consequence Caroline and I gradually saw less of each other over the next year, slowly the gap between our calls got longer, and the suggestions to meet up got fewer, until one day I realised that we had lost contact altogether, and am pretty sure that this was Tim's influence but I could be wrong about that.

I sometimes think about whether our day out is one of the stories told by Caroline at dinner parties, late in the evening when guests and hosts have consumed too much alcohol. It would be nice to think that I can give joy to my friends (even former friends), and to be able to give a laugh to the wider world is no bad thing.

Oh, and in case you are interested, I got the all clear, no STI's for me.

Why on earth are they still single?

Rose likes blokes, not the shave in the morning, go to work in a shirt, use deodorant, knows his own phone number type man, but blokes, the troubled, shower once a week, spend every day in the pub, several children, no regular work, shout in the street, the world's out to get me type bloke.

I maintain this is because Rose has a great life, with no drama, and these guy's have it in wheelbarrow loads.

In the last year she has met several of these charmers online, and this year alone they have been the bloke who called to ask if she would like him to bring her something to drink, wine was requested, but he arrived with half a can of lager for them to share.

The one who arrived, asked to borrow a tenner, which she gave him (!!) had to 'pop out', and never came back.

The bloke she stayed over with, who asked the next morning if she wanted a cooked breakfast; she was delighted her conquest was offering to cook for her. He popped his head around the door to say he had to go out but breakfast was on the table.

Smiling to herself she went to the kitchen to find a carrier bag he had left her contained a couple of rashers of bacon (raw and unwrapped), an egg, a slice of bread and a tin of beans, and a note saying 'Have this one on me x'.

The man who arrived to take her out stumbling drunk but who had definitely only had one.

The one she had been chatting to for a few months or so, who went on holiday, and disappeared for two months. She tried calling, texting, facetiming, Whatsapp-ing, during which time she heard nothing.

Eventually a text message came through saying 'This is Zac's uncle, he hasn't been in touch, as he went missing in Spain'. Rose was distressed and asked questions, which the uncle didn't have any answers to, but he assured her not to worry too much, the police were doing all they could, but he would let her know if anything happened.

Two days later Zac's Instagram account showed him on holiday with his girlfriend and child.

And last but by no means least, the one that probably persuaded Rose to shut down her account with the site – the man who poo'd on her sofa.

Top Five Worst Christmas Presents

At Number Five we have a gesture that is quite sweet, but not as a main Christmas present, we have a Spatula 'to help us remember cooking Fajitas together'.

Close on the Spatula's heels At Number Four we have a leather bag for a vegan girlfriend... Ooh no, you really messed that one up guy!

It's the trusty vacuum cleaner at Number Three ('but it's what I see you do most!', 'that doesn't make it my hobby!!').

Just missing out on the top spot we have the 'almost engagement ring' - as she opened it he changed his mind about proposing, as he 'couldn't face getting married' and told her it was a friendship ring (three years and a house into the relationship).

And finally at Number One surely a present only Morticia Adams could love, (given to a professional pianist in 2015), yes, it's an original 1970's Piano Organ. Straight from someone's garage, it comes with its own family of spiders, and a permanent smell of damp.

Too big to be wrapped in traditional paper, this beauty is presented covered in an old stained sheet.

Thank you for reading Down With Frogs -

I hope that you have enjoyed it,

as a new writer I would appreciate
you leaving me a review; so that other
readers can find their way to my work.

You can follow me on

Blog: https://edengrugerwriter.wordpress.com

Facebook: @edengrugerwriter

Twitter: @edengrugerwrit1